Three Little Kittens Lost Their Mittens

Written and Illustrated by

Elaine Livermore

Houghton Mifflin Company Boston

To John
April and Will
Mike and Jamie
Elizabeth
Billy
Faith
and
Heather

Library of Congress Cataloging in Publication Data

Livermore, Elaine.
    Three little kittens lost their mittens.

    SUMMARY: Three little kittens lose their mittens while
playing and the reader must help find them.
    [1. Stories in rhyme.   2. Cats – Fiction]   I. Title.
PZ8.3.L747Th   [E]   79-12709

ISBN 0-395-28379-5

P   10 9 8 7 6 5 4 3 2

Three Little Kittens
Lost Their Mittens

Three little kittens

Got up one day,

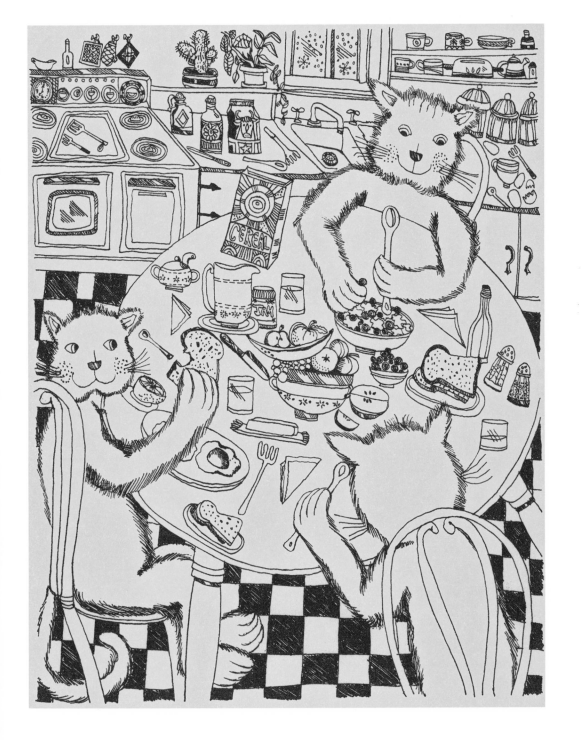

Put on their mittens

And went out to play.

They had ice cream first thing,

Then found books to read,

Used the slide and the swing,

Watched the animals feed.

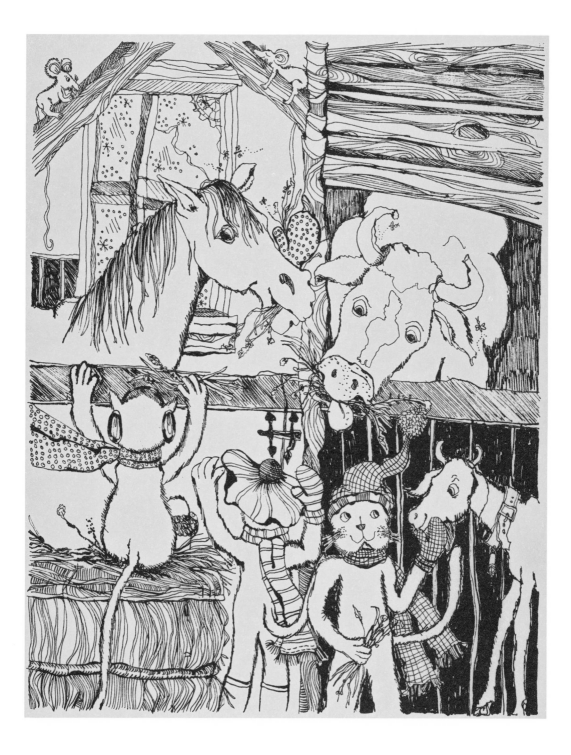

They went to a store,

Then downhill went whizzing,

Headed homeward once more,

But their mittens were missing.

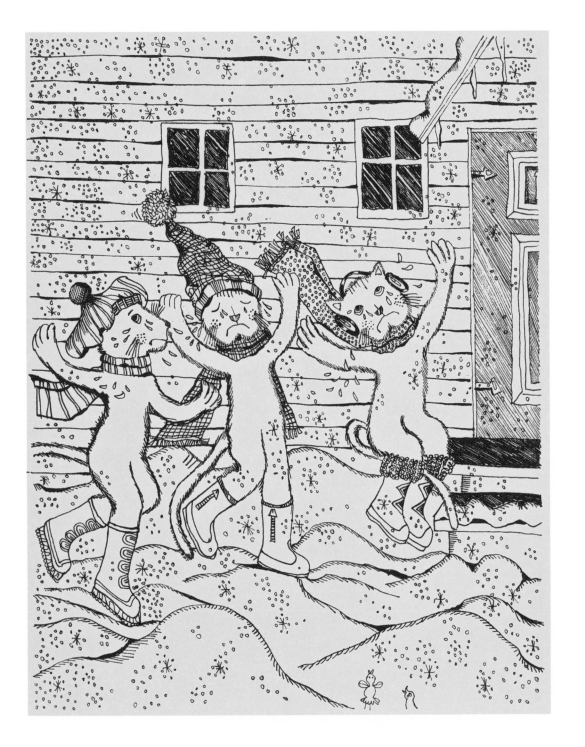

"We lost our mittens!
Oh what shall we do?"
*"You naughty kittens!
No pie for you."*

Oh where could they be?
Can *you* help the kittens?
Please will you go back
And look for their mittens.